ISBN-13:978-1539677925
ISBN-10:1539677923

To Charlotte,

You make me so very proud,

Love Nicky
xx

Acknowledgements

Books are such special things, they have a magical ability to bury into our hearts and souls, allowing us to learn about things, places and ourselves. My love of books has been one which spans years, and some of my favourites still sit on my book shelf. My dream to create my own books has been a long one, but it wasn't until I found my destination that they came to life, and even then they sat in my imagination for so long. I am delighted to be able to create the Adventures of Brian and bring the magic of books and the wonders of therapeutic storytelling together to offer a combination of stories and support to children and their families. Before we start this special story there is thanks to be given;

To my Mum and Dad, who have given me the encouragement to move forward with a dream of creating stories to help small people. Thank you for standing by me, encouraging me and sharing these precious moments.

To Richard for your belief and encouragement that there was a set of books inside me that should be written, this shiny diamond is very grateful.

To my nan and grandad, who forever guide me to follow this path that I am on and to ensure that I stay true to my dreams.

To Veronica, thank you for allowing me the privilege of naming Brian after Brian. There is a sprinkling of him all over this book.

To my beautiful Charlotte, you are loved so much..

I hope you enjoy these books as much as I have enjoyed writing them

Love Nicky x x

This book belongs to:

....

It was a sunny morning and Brian was playing in the garden with his favourite ball when his mummy came outside. She had the car keys in her hand and called to him "are you coming in the car Brian?"

Brian looked at her and tilted his head, he wondered where she was going?

"Do you want to come to the seaside?" she asked.

Brian had never been to the seaside, what if he didn't like it? He got that funny feeling in his tummy that made him want to run and hide under his blanket. The feeling got stronger so he ran to his bed, dived under the blanket and peeped out. The feeling made Brian worried, it made him feel a little bit scared and upset, he didn't like it and wanted to stay near his mummy.

"Come on Brian, what's wrong?" his mummy said following him into the house.

Brian hid under his blanket but peeped his head out and looked at his mummy….. The funny feeling made him feel worried, he didn't like it.

"Don't you want to come to the seaside Brian?" his mummy asked as she stroked his head. Brian crawled a little way out from under his blanket and looked up at her with his big green eyes… "If you were to come you could have lots of fun, and Boo is coming too!" she said.

Brian thought about it for a moment, if Boo was coming then he probably could have fun… but the funny feeling was still in his tummy and the thought of a new place still made him worried. He slowly crawled out from under his blanket and snuggled up to his mummy. Maybe he could try….

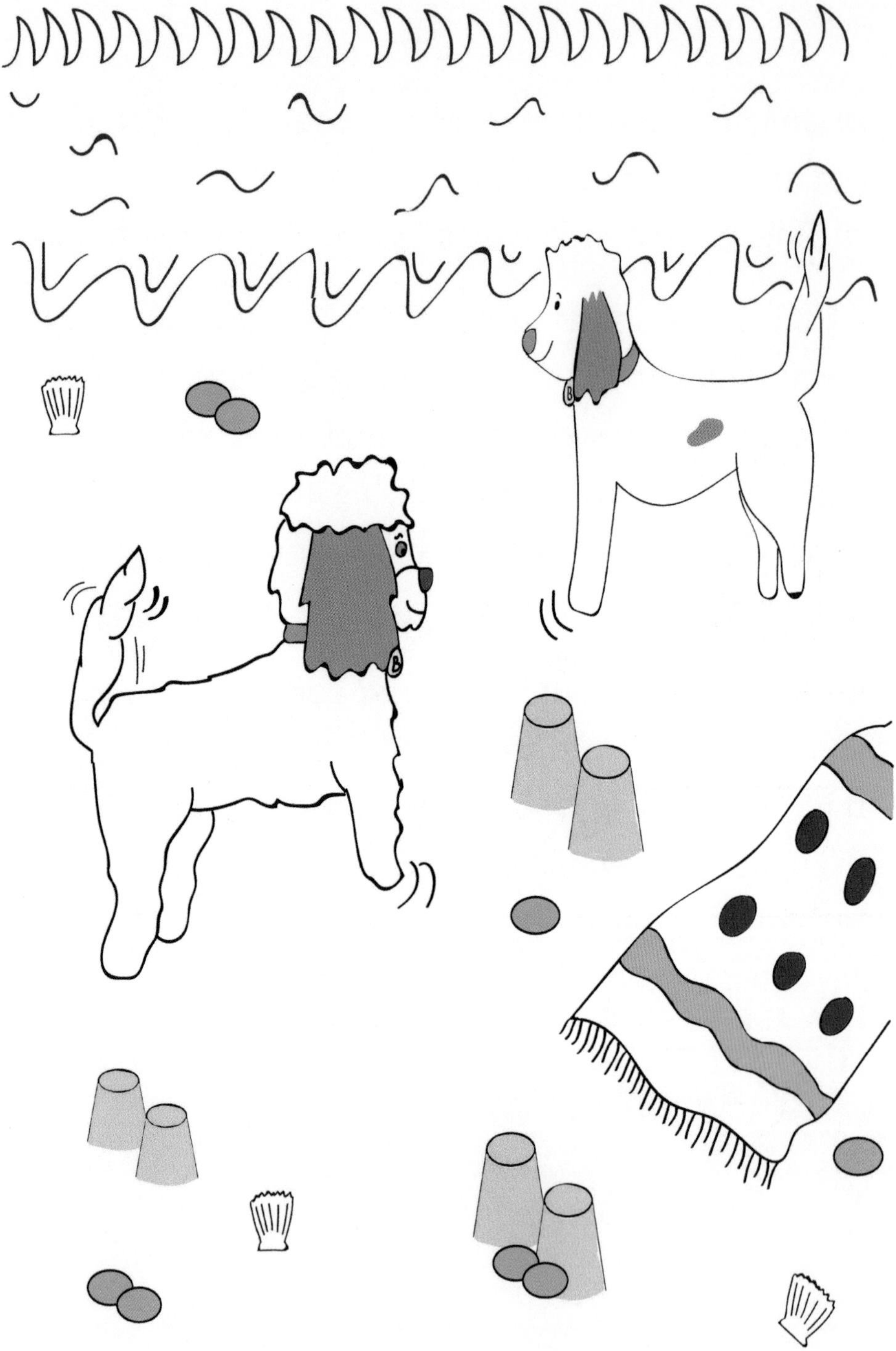

Brian jumped in the car and they drove to the seaside place. When they got there, it was very big. Brian felt the funny feeling come back, it swished about in his tummy, he really didn't like it. He hid behind his mummy, he just wanted to go home.

He was just looking at his mummy's towel and wondering if he could hide under it when Boo came running towards him! Brian forgot about the funny feeling for a moment and leapt up and ran around in circles with his best friend. "Brian!" Boo yelped loudly at him!

"Boo! You're here!" Brian replied. Boo stopped bouncing about and took a long hard look at Brian. "Are you ok?" she asked.

"Oh Boo, I have a horrid swishy funny feeling in my tummy... I don't like new places!" Brian replied.

"But Brian, the seaside is fun! There's sand that moves when you walk, the sea is great fun and if we are good I think our mummies might even buy us an ice cream!" Boo said.

Brian liked the idea of an ice cream and the sea sounded fun... "The funny feeling makes me feel all worried though" he replied.

"Maybe you could come and play for a little while and you might find that it gets better?" Boo suggested.

Brian thought about it, he could play for a little while and see if it got better? One of the things he loved, was that when he played with Boo he often felt happier, so maybe he would find that he felt better..

"Ok, I'll try" Brian said to Boo.

"Great! Let's go and play in the sea!" she yelped and ran towards the water, Brian hesitated for a moment and then ran after her feeling the swishy sand under his feet, it really did feel nice...

They played in the sea and swished their paws in the sand and after a little while his mummy bought him an ice cream, he snuggled up next to her and as he licked the ice cream he noticed that the funny feeling in his tummy wasn't so big now.

The next morning Brian was laying on his mummy's bed looking out of the window when he saw Blue Butterfly float past. He jumped off the bed and carefully ran downstairs and out into the garden.

"Blue Butterfly! Blue Butterfly! Stop! I need you!" he shouted after her.

Blue Butterfly hovered in the sky and then floated down to her flower.

"Hello Brian, what's wrong? You sound upset" she said.

"Oh Blue Butterfly, I need your help. I Have a feeling and I cannot make it go away!" Brian was so upset that a little tear fell out of his eye and rolled down his fur.

"Oh Brian, don't cry, tell me all about it and we can make it better" Blue Butterfly replied.

Brian sat down on the grass next to Blue Butterfly's flower and started to explain:

"Sometimes, when Mummy tells me we are going to new places I get this funny feeling in my body. It starts off small and gets bigger and bigger. It makes me feel worried and a little bit shaky and then I just want to hide under my blanket where it's safe" Brian told her.

"Oh Brian, you have nerves!" Blue Butterfly told him.

Brian sat up straight and tilted his head as he listened to what she was saying. "Nerves? What are nerves?" he asked.

"Sometimes, when we are visiting new places, or meeting new people, or trying something new it can make us feel nervous. Nerves are a way that our body tells us that we need to be careful, maybe we need to learn something new, or listen more, but when we get used to the new place they start to go away" Blue Butterfly explained.

"So my feelings are normal?" Brian asked, looking a little bit surprised.

"Yes! They are just your body telling you that you are going to do a new thing. Sometimes the nerves get a bit confused with the excited feelings and they get mixed up. Would you like me to teach you a way to make them feel better?" Blue Butterfly asked.

"Could you? That would be really good! Then I could go and have fun with my mummy again" Brian replied. "Of course I can! It's very simple. Are you ready?" Blue Butterfly said. She spread her wings out and hovered in the air above Brian, then very gently sat on his head.

Brian looked up at Blue Butterfly who was now sat between his ears on the top of his head. "What are you doing?" Brian asked. "I'm going to teach you a way to feel braver!" Blue Butterfly said sounding very excited.

Brian wondered why she had to sit on his head to do this but decided to let her just teach, he had never had a butterfly on his head before!

Blue Butterfly began… "Right Brian, stand up straight!" she said. Brian did his best standing.

"What you need to do is imagine a line on the floor in front of you" she told him.

Brian looked at the grass and decided that his line would be yellow like the sunshine. He imagined the line stretched out on the grass in front of him. "Got it!" Brian said.

"Great, well done. Now, I want you to think about something that worries you and let the funny feeling come back so that we can let it go" she said.

Brian thought about it, he didn't like new places so he pictured a new place and felt the funny feeling creeping back "It's back!" he yelped. "Ok now Brian I want you to throw the feeling in the air above your head and then jump over the line and get away from it as quickly as you can!" Blue Butterfly said really loudly!

Brian jumped, she was very loud! He used all his strength and pushed the funny feeling up out of his body into the air and did his best jumping and leapt over the line!

"Well done Brian!" Blue Butterfly said. "Did you hear that big thump as it hit the floor! How are you feeling now?"

Brian stopped for a minute, he had heard the funny feeling hit the floor and when he thought about it he noticed that the funny feeling wasn't in his body anymore! He ran around in a circle and jumped from side to side – it was gone! "Blue Butterfly! It's gone!'" he said.

Blue Butterfly sat back on her flower and smiled, "Good work Brian, now you know that the sooner you throw the feeling up in the air and jump forward the sooner you will feel better!"

Brian was so happy! Now he knew what to do! "Thank you Blue Butterfly!" he said running around the garden as fast as he could!

The next day Brian was playing in the house with his favourite toy duck when his mummy came in. "Brian, would you like to go to a party?" she asked.

Brian stopped, he looked at his mummy, then at his toy duck and then felt the funny feeling in his body..... oh no!

As he was about to run to his bed to hide under the blanket he remembered what Blue Butterfly had taught him!

He stood up really straight and then looked at the floor and drew his bright yellow line, as bright as the sunshine. He imagined the line stretched out on the rug in front of him.

Then Brian thought of the funny feeling which was creeping back, then he used all his strength and threw the feeling in the air above his head and did his best jumping – he jumped over the line to get away from it as quickly as he could!

As Brian landed on the rug over his line he stopped for a minute, he had heard the funny feeling hit the floor, then he thought about the party and he noticed that the funny feeling wasn't in his body anymore!

He ran around in a circle and jumped up to his mummy! "Would you like to come to the party?" she asked him again.

Now the feeling was gone he really did! Brian leapt up and gave her a big kiss and then ran to the kitchen to have his lead put on so they could go!

Brian had so much fun at the party and played with his friends and stole the ham sandwiches off the table! When he got home that night he was so tired that he curled up under his blanket and fell fast asleep.

The next day he was playing with his toys when he saw Blue Butterfly float past the window. He ran outside to tell her all about the party!

Blue Butterfly sat on her flower and listened to Brian's story and when he had finished she said; "Did you notice how good you felt when you threw the funny feeling away?". Brian thought about it, it really did - feel good - when he threw the funny feeling away! "I had much more fun after I let the funny feeling go" he told her.

"You can try anything you want now Brian, because you have learnt how to let the feeling go. You might have already noticed that the more you practice letting it go, the quicker it leaves!" she said. Brian smiled, Blue Butterfly was right, the more he practiced letting the funny feeling go – the quicker it left!

"One of the things you will love about throwing it away, is how much more fun you can have in new places now!" Blue Butterfly said, then she stretched her wings and flew into the sky.

As Brian snuggled in his bed that afternoon for his nap he thought about what Blue Butterfly had taught him.... He felt much happier now he knew.

So now Brian knows that if the funny feeling appears he just needs to stand up really straight, draw a line on the floor, then concentrate really hard and throw the funny feeling in the air above his head and then jump over the line and get away from it as quickly as he can!

And he always remembers that the sooner he throws the feeling up in the air and jumps forward the sooner he will feel better!

Keep jumping!

X

Other books in this series:

Brian and the Blue Butterfly

Brian and the Magic Night

Brian and the Black Pebble

Brian and the Christmas Wish

Brian and the Shiny Star

Brian and the Naughty Day

Brian and the Funny Feeling

Nicky lives in Sussex with Brian the Cockapoo where they enjoy daily adventures with friends and family. Nicky started her career by spending 10 years working in the early years sector with 0-5 year olds before lecturing in early years and health and social care to students aged 16 and over. She later retrained as a hypnotherapist and now runs A Step at a Time Hypnotherapy working with children and adults to resolve their personal issues.

The Adventures of Brian books were the development of a dream of wanting to offer parents of young children tools and resources to support their children to manage worries and fears in a non-intrusive way. Having spent a large part of her career reading stories at all speeds and in all voices this collection of storybooks was born.

Each book in the collection covers a different worry which affects children on a day to day basis and uses therapeutic storytelling to support children in resolving these through Brian's daily adventures.

You can find more titles in the Adventures of Brian series by visiting:

www.adventuresofbrian.co.uk

Printed in Great Britain
by Amazon